KU-342-817

THE
MAGIC
HOUR

IAN BECK

For Juliet Trewellard

First published 2019 by order of the Tate Trustees
by Tate Publishing, a division of Tate Enterprises Ltd,
Millbank, London SW1P 4RG
www.tate.org.uk/publishing

Text and illustrations © Ian Beck, 2019

First published 2019

All rights reserved. No part of this book may be reprinted or utilised in any form or by any
electronic, mechanical or other means, now known or hereafter invented, including photocopying
and recording, or in any information storage or retrieval system, without permission in writing
from the publishers or a licence from the Copyright Licensing Agency Ltd, www.cla.co.uk

A catalogue record for this book is available from the British Library

ISBN 978 1 84976 624 1

Distributed in the United States and Canada by ABRAMS, New York
Library of Congress Control Number applied for
Printed and bound in China by Toppan Leefung Printing Ltd
Colour Reproduction by DL Imaging Ltd, London

Lily was eleven that hot summer long ago, and Rose was nine.

The best thing about the old house they were staying in was the wonderful garden.
It twisted all the way down to a slow and sleepy river.

They went everywhere together.   First Lily, then Rose.

Along the paths with their long hair flying. They were never still.
"Wait for me," Rose would call out as they ran.

On the brightest, hottest days they played in the shade of the old oak tree. In and out of the leafy shadows they swung.

First Lily, then Rose.

"You'll just have to wait your turn," Lily said.

The sun shone every day. It grew hotter and hotter,
until one afternoon Mother cut their hair.

First Lily, then Rose.

"That's better," she said. "You'll feel much cooler now.
Off you go out to play and try not to argue."

Early one evening, Rose climbed
so high up the oak tree that she could
see right into the garden
of the bigger house next door.

Something
caught
her eye.

In the wooded glade down
by the river, a small golden light
was flickering.
"What can that be?" she wondered.

She wanted to follow the light, but Mother interrupted her thoughts.
"Lily, Rose, supper time!"

"Bother," said Rose as she climbed down again.

All through supper, Rose wondered about the
flickering light.

At bedtime, as they watched the sun go down, Rose could
keep her secret no longer.

She whispered to Lily,
"I saw something today from the top of the tree…"
"What was it?" asked Lily.
"A fairy!" exclaimed Rose. "Over there in the big garden."
"Are you sure it was a fairy?" said Lily.
"Quite sure. It was teeny tiny and all bright and shiny,
and it was fluttering all over the place."

"Let's go and see if it's still there!"
said Lily.

They crept
down the stairs.
First Lily,
then Rose.

As quietly as they could, they squeezed through the scratchy hedge and into the garden next door. All was silver and blue in the moonlight.

A mist was rising up from
the river. They stared and
stared until they had to blink.
"Look over there!" gasped Rose.
"Now there's another one!"

Sure enough, there were now two points of golden light flickering in the mist.

Wide-eyed, they watched as the lights moved closer.

It was Rose who dared to step out first.

"Listen," she whispered, as a stream of beautiful music washed over them,

"fairies singing!"

And for a moment, time seemed to stand still.

Then out of the mist two figures appeared.

"Hallo there," said a kind voice. "Where have you two come from?
I thought at first you were two little ghosts."

"Oh," said Rose, "your lanterns, we thought we had seen fairy lights
and heard their magical song."

"Those are the nightingales singing," said the
woman. "They always sing at twilight."

"We've been out
painting," said the man.
"Painting at night?" said Lily.

"We call this the magic hour."
said the man.

"The light is very special and makes
everything look enchanted in the
early summer."

"The magic hour?"
said Rose and Lily together.

25

"Look at the way light shines on your white dresses,"
said the woman, as they walked the the girls home.
"And see how it makes the flowers look blue-white.
There are lilies and roses scattered in the long grass,"
she added.
"I'm called Rose," said Rose.
"And my name is Lily," said Lily.

When they reached the gate between the gardens there was Mother,
looking worried. "Wherever have you been, girls?" she exclaimed.
"You gave me quite a fright."
"I saw a fairy," said Rose.
"We were out painting and the girls saw our lanterns," said the man.
"They must have heard the nightingales too."
As if on cue, another peal of silvery birdsong rang out.

Before bedtime, Lily and Rose looked out of the open window
across the moonlit garden.
"We didn't find your fairy,"
said Lily.

"But we did hear the nightingales," said Rose,
"and it was the most beautiful song in the world."
"I know there are fairies hiding in the woods," she whispered.
"Let's go and look for them
again tomorrow!"

Carnation, Lily, Lily, Rose 1885 – 6

This painting was created by John Singer Sargent and is set in a garden in the Cotswolds village of Broadway. The two young girls, Dolly and Polly Barnard, are lighting Japanese lanterns with tapers. Singer Sargent loved to paint dusk, or "the magic hour", when the light was just right. The painting can be seen at Tate Britain, London.

When I first visited the Tate Gallery (Tate Britain) as a callow art student my favourite painting in the collection was Carnation Lily Lily Rose by John Singer Sargent. My taste has remained remarkably steady but I would never have guessed then that well over fifty years later I would have been asked to thread a story and pictures around the twilight mood of this wonderful painting.

Ian Beck